# Pass the Jam, Jim!

# Pass the Jam, Jim

Kaye Umansky &
Margaret Chamberlain

TED SMART

Hurry Mabel, lay that table!

Jane, put Wayne back in his pram!

Where's the bread, Fred?
Bread I said, Fred.

Pass the jam, Jim,
Jam, Jim, jam.

Cut the cake,
Kate.

Pour the tea,
Lee.

Who wants cheese and who wants ham?

Pass the pot, Dot.
Is it hot, Dot?

Pass the jam, Jim,
Jam, Jim, jam.

Here's the salt, Walt.
Use your spoon, June.

Jill don't spill
And Phil don't cram!

What a mess, Bess,
On your dress, Bess.

Pass the jam, Jim,
Jam, Jim, jam.

Drink your juice,
Bruce.

Slice of pie,
Guy?

Sip your soup up slowly, Sam.

Who's for custard?
Where's the mustard?

Pass the jam, Jim,
Jam, Jim, jam.

Boil the kettle, Gretel.

Bring the butter, Betty.

Charles wants chips and so does Pam.

Thanks a lot, Jim . . .
Oh! You've NOT, Jim!

JIM! YOU'VE EATEN
ALL THE JAM!

0 370 32911 2

This edition produced for The Book People Ltd,
Hall Wood Avenue, Haydock, St Helens, WA11 9UL

First published in Great Britain by Random House Children's Books 2000
The Book People edition published 2006

Red Fox Books are published by Random House Children's Books,
61-63 Uxbridge Road, London W5 5SA,
a division of The Random House Group Ltd,
in Australia by Random House Australia (Pty) Ltd,
20 Alfred Street, Milsons Point, Sydney, NSW 2061, Australia
in New Zealand by Random House New Zealand Ltd,
18 Poland Road, Glenfield, Auckland 10, New Zealand
and in South Africa by Random House (Pty) Ltd,
Endulini, 5A Jubilee Road, Parktown 2193, South Africa

THE RANDOM HOUSE GROUP Limited Reg No. 954009
www.**kids**at**randomhouse**.co.uk

A CIP catalogue record for this book is available from the British Library.

Printed in Singapore

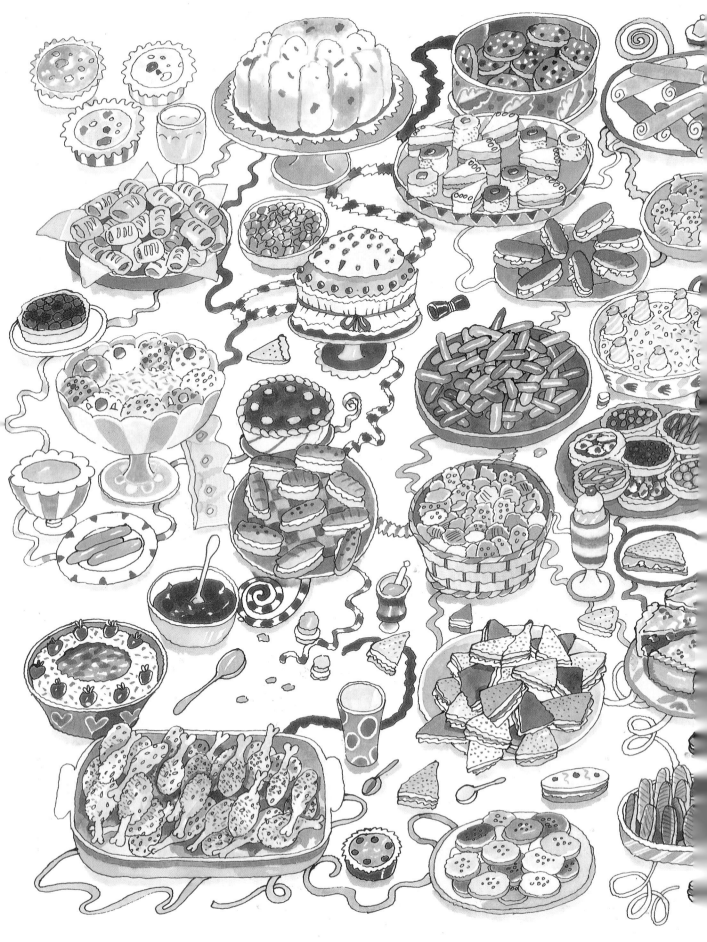